SHORT STORY COLLECTIONS BY JIM HEYNEN

The Youngest Boy
(Holy Cow! Press, 2021)

Ordinary Sins: Stories
(Milkweed Editions, 2014)

Old Swayback
(Midnight Paper Sales, 2006)

The Boys' House: New & Selected Stories
(Minnesota Historical Society Press, 2001)

The One-Room Schoolhouse: Stories About the Boys
(A. Knopf, 1993; Vintage Contemporaries, 1994)

You Know What Is Right
(North Point Press, 1985)

The Man Who Kept Cigars In His Cap
(Graywolf Press, 1979)

Please visit *www.jimheynen.com*
for a complete listing of published work

the YOUNGEST BOY

STORIES

by JIM HEYNEN

with ILLUSTRATIONS

by TOM POHRT

PREFACE

by DAVID PICHASKE

HOLY COW! PRESS
Duluth, Minnesota

2021

Cover art and illustrations by Tom Pohrt.
Preface by David Pichaske.
Author photograph: circa 1950, hand-tinted, photographer unknown.
Book and cover design by Anton Khodakovsky.

Printed and bound in the United States.

First printing, Spring, 2021.

ISBN 978-1513645599
Library of Congress Control Number: 2020949331
10 9 8 7 6 5 4 3 2 1

Holy Cow! Press projects are funded in part by grant awards from the
Ben and Jeanne Overman Charitable Trust, the Elmer L. and Eleanor J.
Andersen Foundation, the Lenfestey Family Foundation, Schwegman
Lundberg & Woessner, P.A., and by gifts from generous individual
donors. We are grateful to Springboard for the Arts for their support
as our fiscal sponsor.

Holy Cow! Press books are distributed to the trade by Consortium
Book Sales & Distribution, c/o Ingram Publisher Services, Inc., 210
American Drive, Jackson, TN 38301.

For inquiries, please write to: *Holy Cow! Press*, Post Office Box 3170,
Mount Royal Station, Duluth, MN 55803.
Visit *www.holycowpress.org*

Contents

PREFACE

by DAVID PICHASKE

OVER THE COURSE of his impressive career, Jim Heynen has given us novels, poems, a handbook for writers, the text for a coffee table book of barn photos, even a book of interviews with *One Hundred Over 100,* but he is best known for his collections of short fiction: *The Man Who Kept Cigars in His Cap, The One-Room Schoolhouse, You Know What Is Right, The Boys' House.* These tales chronicle the running battle of young farm boys against old men, city folk, each other, Nature and human nature. In this new collection—illustrated by Tom Pohrt, whose art graced some of Heynen's previous books—he turns our attention again to the farm kids, especially to the youngest farm kid.

The stories are short, what James Thurber once called "fables for our times," what I once called "Parables of Innocence and Experience." And they are set in the 1950s, over half a century ago. The man who has lived all across northern America (with time abroad); whose graduate studies involved studies in Milton and the Renaissance poets; who has taught at nearly a dozen different colleges and universities . . . this man derives much of his own best material from memories of grades one through eight in a one-room school house near Sioux Center, Iowa. "In my hands," he has written, "there still lives a farmer." Number 25 of Heynen's on-line "Fifty Hints for Fiction Writers" is this: "Any time you feel the well is dry, write about your first thirteen years—they are your only inexhaustible source." These years are certainly his inexhaustible source—his time and his place. "An old barn is layered with stories," Heynen wrote in *Harker's Barns,* everything from father-son arguments to individuals experiencing first romantic encounters. Heynen is at heart a writer of place, in that for him place determines character and vision, and our early years are the bedrock of that vision. Bob Dylan once told *Playboy*, "I'm North Dakota-Minnesota-Midwestern. My brains and feelings have come from there." Heynen himself once wrote that having lived "close to nature and its creatures" may be "the most essential difference" between his own art and that of other writers.

One reviewer of the 1985 collection of boys' stories, *You Know What Is Right,* observed that for Heynen, mental consciousness is formed by physical confrontations with the world around us. This does not, however, make him a mud-on-the-shoes realist: his experiences and thus his stories occasionally drift into the surreal. (Dylan also once pointed out that you can have plenty of surreal experiences just looking out of your window at a Minnesota winter.) Being close to their place and time, Heynen's boys are in touch with the physical world. They survive without toilet paper and are not tangled up in complex technologies: they use simple machines, they watch little TV, and of course they have no Facebook pages. They view pretentious, fancy pants, high-falootin' city folk as way too far over the top, disconnected from the world and thus from themselves.

Simplicity is truth. The youngest boy especially understands this. Yesterday's lesson was suck it up and do the work. (Listen up here, folks.) Today's lesson is we all need a dog. (Get yourself a dog—humans and animals are in this together.) A daily lesson: Find your own faucet. And while you can and should imagine, dreams and books don't get the job done. Daydreams are not real. Thinking will not let you fly over the schoolhouse. In the end, the real world wins every time. Back off the socializing and look at Nature. Life is amazing.

This is not to say that Nature is always benevolent. Back in the 1980 edition of the Gale Literature reference series *Contemporary Authors,* Heynen told us, "I am interested in developing a distinctively rural American aesthetic, one which I would not call a sentimental realism, but rather a clear and even harsh acceptance of the earth and animal presence in our historical and contemporary lives." He has long recognized the dark side of Nature . . . and of human nature. There are pretty pigeons out there, but there are also hawks. There are skunks. Around my house, coyotes howl at night. Animals and people both have a light and a dark side, as we learn in this collection's first story. Chickens peck at other chickens. The older men castrate and dehorn animals, chop the tail off Skippy just to keep him from chasing his own tail around, and eventually kill him at age four because they suspect he killed a neighbor's chickens. But in the end, there is a purpose to Nature: a crow feeds on a road-killed rabbit; cows, hogs, and chickens die to put bread on the table. We may try, like the youngest boy, to cover for the rat that stole an ear of corn, to block the chickens' pecking, to help the rooster escape execution, to convince Texas hunters to use clay pigeons instead of live pigeons, but we're not always successful. And, as the youngest boy learns, bad mixes with good. And that's good. Cow manure, the old saying goes, "smells like money." Town kids, who are obsessed with nice teeth and nice clothes, can't see the value of cow shit, but farm kids can. Besides, the youngest boy realizes, manure is what makes the corn and oats grow, and dried cow droppings smell good when they burn. The main character of Heynen's *Cosmos Coyote and William the Nice* calls this "a battleground of contradictions." In this book, the lesson is co-existence. The mission of the youngest boy may be kindness and justice, perhaps because he is close to and sympathetic with animals and understands their pain and their joy both, but just looking at the birds he is developing a complex consciousness.

Often Heynen's fables end with a brief moral lesson, just in case we missed the story's point. Heynen wants us to learn our lessons, and on at least one occasion he challenged, "You write the moral to this story." The interesting thing about Heynen's lessons is that the story may be set somewhere in 1950s rural Iowa, but the lesson applies to all of us today. Teresa Jordan once noted that Heynen's stories speak to "our own memories, whether we be male or female, urban or rural." Some of these lessons are especially important to our times, because we have lost touch with Nature and human nature. One rooster is very good at waking people up around five a.m.; his successor is "second-best and couldn't crow anybody awake, not even when flapping his wings." Some chickens lay an egg every day; others do not. In real life, everyone doesn't get a medal. On the other hand, damaged people teach life lessons on what not to do to get damaged. And a woman with just one arm may be perfectly capable of picking apples and safety-pinning her own shirt. The storm you prepared for at great lengths may not come. That fire alert might have been "just for practice." Birth, although messy and even traumatic, has an unspoken beauty that may be lost to people locked in a digital world. So quit the talk, talk, talk and spend some time with baby pigs. Check out the older hogs and cattle. Look at the beautiful sunset. A work of art, even if it is beautiful, may end up tucked in the clothes closet behind some clothes. (Don't fret—it'll be there for years.)

The very idea that stories teach a lesson is refreshing in a post-postmodern world, where nothing makes any sense because—all too often—the author's intent was to not make any sense, just to be clever and entertaining. Jim Heynen shows us that we can be entertained and instructed both . . . and that even the experiences of Iowa farm kids can be archetypal. The lessons, incidentally, are quite valid: It turns out that fires of dried cow pies do smell good—I learned that my year in Outer Mongolia.

These stories are entertaining (readers familiar with Heynen's earlier books will enjoy being transported back to the man who kept cigars in his cap, and to the boys who collected pocket gopher feet and marveled over the mystery of Girls), but in a world that is increasingly mechanized, dissociated from place, and cut off from Nature and human nature, Heynen's message needs to be heard. "Something is going too fast nowadays," he wrote in *The One-Room Schoolhouse*; things have only speeded up, and we need to recognize the problem. At the time of these stories, tractors were replacing workers, and bales of straw meant the end of straw stacks; today computers replace people and digital music means nobody plays piano. We need to recover ourselves and preserve our selves. That, if anything, is the lesson of the coronavirus lock-down, which threatens to turn us into a generation of Zoombies. Your phone is not the world. Listen to Heynen. Take a look at that sunset out there! Spend more time with your dog—he can teach you a lot about peaceful coexistence! Reclaim that perfectly good pencil someone tossed out in the trash. Don't let that squirrel be the only one who knows what's going on out there. Slow down, people! It's a beautiful world.

Taking Sides

O N THE FARM where the youngest boy lived there were too many animals to count.

There was a hoghouse full of sows and feeder pigs and a boar or two. Some squeals came from their direction now and then, but they settled their own arguments. There was a cattle feedlot full of steers. All they did was eat cracked corn and molasses to get fat for market. There was a chicken coop full of fluttering laying hens and two roosters. The laying hens talked in their clucking way to the youngest boy when he gathered their eggs. The roosters didn't say anything until five in the morning when the loudest one woke everybody up. That rooster stopped waking people the day he was butchered. The other rooster stepped up, but he was second-best and couldn't crow anybody awake, not even when he flapped his wings as if that would make his crowing louder.

Then there were the cows who spent their time chewing their way across the pasture until they got called to the barn where stanchions locked their heads to make them stand in one place while they were milked.

There was one big Holstein bull who spent most of his time in the feedlot walking around and eating with the steers. Now and then the men put that big bull out in the pasture with the cows. The men never told the youngest boy why they did that, but the youngest boy noticed that the bull looked happier when he was back to the lazy life of eating with the steers.

As the youngest boy understood things, all of those farm animals put bread on the table. They bought new shoes, new shirts, new everything. There wouldn't be a car to ride to church in without those farm animals. There wouldn't be Christmas presents!

So all those animals meant money, but what about the pigeons and sparrows and barn swallows, the crows and blackbirds and brown thrashers and robins? And the owl that hooted everyone to sleep at night? The grown-ups said all those birds were nice, even if they didn't put bread on the table. They were frosting on the cake.

Sometimes the men talked about nuisance animals. Those were the little critters they called pests or rodents, or both.

If he had to be an animal, the youngest boy wasn't sure which one he would be. Sometimes he thought it would be fun to be a rooster and wake people up when they didn't feel like waking up. Sometimes a pig lying in the mud looked like more fun than sitting at the table for supper. He wouldn't want to be a cow with her head locked in a stanchion while the milkers took what they could get.

But then there was the rodent rat the youngest boy watched eating kernels off a big ear of corn. The rat took all the kernels and left nothing but a corncob.

That same rat sniffed out a rattrap in the corncrib alleyway and ran around it to go off for another nuisance adventure.

On some days, even a rat needed somebody to take his side. The youngest boy picked up the corncob and dropped it in the cattle feedlot so the rat wouldn't get the blame. Nobody would blame a steer for eating corn. But if I were a rat, he wondered, would anybody take my side now and then?

TOWN KIDS

SOME TOWN KIDS came to visit the farm. They wanted to see the baby pigs. Three sows had just littered, so showing them baby pigs was easy.

"Can I hold one?"

The youngest boy got into the farrowing pen with the tamest sow, a big Chester White. She had ten little white pigs to choose from. The youngest boy picked up one that wasn't nursing.

"How about this one?" he said and handed it to one of the town kids.

Town kids always did and said the same thing when they held a baby pig. They put their chin down on the head of the baby pig and said, "They're so cute. So cute." That's exactly what this town kid did and said, but then added, "Take a picture." But nobody had a camera.

When they left the sows and baby pigs, the youngest boy showed them the feedlots where the hogs and cattle were eating or just lying around. None of the town kids said "so cute" anymore. The animals looked dirty to them, and there wasn't any spot in the hog and cattle lots where an animal had not gone to the toilet. The town kids didn't even want to walk out there where the animals spent most of their day. The dirt looked awfully bumpy and they could tell by the color that most of the bumps were more than dirt.

"At the county fair, all the animals look so clean," said one of the town kids.

"And somebody always cleans up behind them."

Out here on the farm, the animals looked dirty and nobody was out there to clean up after them.

"Isn't there a big litter box somewhere that the pigs and cows can use?"

The youngest boy knew something about manure and that manure was what made the corn and oats grow. He also knew what the men meant when the hog and cattle lots were really smelly. The men didn't say the hog and cattle lots smelled terrible. They said they smelled like money.

When one of the town kids said, "How can anybody stand this smell?" the youngest boy repeated what he had heard the men say. He said, "Smells like money to me."

The town kids didn't understand how anyone could say the awful farm smells were the smell of money, but that was the message they had to go home with.

SKIPPY

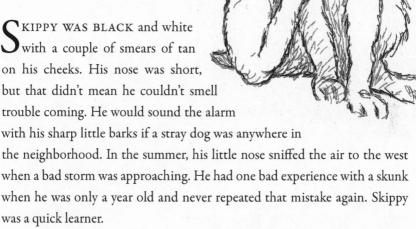

SKIPPY WAS BLACK and white
with a couple of smears of tan
on his cheeks. His nose was short,
but that didn't mean he couldn't smell
trouble coming. He would sound the alarm
with his sharp little barks if a stray dog was anywhere in
the neighborhood. In the summer, his little nose sniffed the air to the west
when a bad storm was approaching. He had one bad experience with a skunk
when he was only a year old and never repeated that mistake again. Skippy
was a quick learner.

Skippy was not a house dog. The only time he was allowed inside
the house was when the temperatures fell below minus-thirty. On nor-
mal winter nights he slept with the cats in the alleyway of the barn.
The heat from the cows in their stanchions on one side and the pens
of calves on the other side made sleeping in the barn for the cats and
Skippy quite comfortable. Skippy and the cats were not bosom buddies
but they didn't give each other any trouble. They slept in different spots
and drank from different water dishes. They were like neighbors who
didn't have anything to talk about so they just left each other alone.

Everybody knew that Skippy preferred to spend his time with the youngest boy and would follow him around the farmyard with his legs pattering alongside. They might stop to look at the pigs or cattle, but Skippy wasn't all that interested in them. Much in the same way that Skippy got along with the cats, he got along with the rest of the farm animals. He didn't have any grievances against them and they didn't have any grievances against him, so they pretty much ignored each other. They had their own version of peaceful coexistence.

Skippy's peaceful coexistence with the animals was no problem until the men expected Skippy to take issue with the pig that broke out of its pen and went roaming around the farmyard like some kind of runaway.

"Sic 'em, Skippy!" one of the men yelled and pointed at the pig that thought it could break out of its pen without any consequences.

Skippy followed the man's finger and obeyed the man by running up to the wayward pig. The pig waited for Skippy with its snout out. The pig's and Skippy's noses touched. They were just saying "hello" and that was all. Skippy looked back at the man with a look that said, "Now what am I supposed to do?"

"Git 'em!" the man yelled and pointed toward the pen where the pig was supposed to go.

Skippy did nothing. He stood firmly on his four little legs and looked at the man as if to say, "If you have an issue with this pig, it's your issue."

Toilet Paper

There wasn't any toilet paper in the outhouse. The grown-ups didn't see any reason to waste money on toilet paper when they had plenty of corncobs and Sears-Roebuck catalogs.

But when the youngest boy went along into town on Saturday nights and went to the bathroom there, toilet paper became one of the magical mysteries that town folks kept to themselves. When he went to the bathroom in town, he didn't use more toilet paper than he needed, but he marveled at its softness and how it rolled out magically from that little toilet-paper hanger on the bathroom walls.

At night on the farm, when he prayed his prayers before going to sleep, he prayed that everyone in the world would have enough to eat, that they would not suffer from terrible illnesses, that they would always give thanks to Him from whom all blessings flowed, and then, almost apologetically, he whispered, "But, Dear God, if it be Your will, please take care of Skippy, and also, if you have time, in your Great Wisdom, please put some toilet paper in the outhouse so that that I can better praise your name. Amen."

CEDAR CHEST

"YOU'RE BIG ENOUGH now that we should be able to trust you to stay here by yourself for a few hours. We'll be back for evening chores. Check the water fountains. Make sure the chickens don't get out. You know what to do and what not to do."

And with that the grown-ups got in the car with the older boys and left the youngest boy on his own. Just him and Skippy. It was a glorious day!

As soon as everyone left the farm, the youngest boy told Skippy to stay right outside the front door. Skippy sat. The youngest boy went straight to the bedroom closets to see what secrets he might find. In the back of a big closet was a cedar chest that he had never checked out. Would it smell like mothballs when he opened it? he wondered. It didn't. Everything inside was packed tight and neatly folded. A tablecloth with lace around the edge. Some orange napkins. The only time he ever saw these things was on Thanksgiving Day. When he dug a little deeper, he found layer after layer of perfectly folded clothes. His eye landed on something that was covered with little red flowers. He held it up. It was a girl's dress. And under it was another girl's dress. Half of the cedar chest was filled with girls' clothing. It didn't take long for the youngest boy to figure out what was going on here. Somebody had wanted a little girl but had gotten only boys boys boys.

The youngest boy held up the pretty dress with the little red flowers and walked to the bedroom mirror. Why not? he thought. He took off his own clothes and slipped into the girl's dress. He went back to the mirror and

looked at himself. He had never looked at his bare legs before. He had nice legs. He turned to the side and looked back over his shoulder. He had a nice neck too. He returned to the cedar chest and dug around some more. He found a girl's hat that was probably meant for Sunday school for the girl who was never born. It was red with a big brim and a cloth flower on the side. There weren't any girls' shoes in the cedar chest so he walked back to the mirror in bare feet and looked at himself. Amazing! The red hat and the red-flowered dress were a good match. He couldn't remember ever seeing a nicer looking girl. If what he was looking at in the mirror were a real girl, he would want to be her friend. Would the grown-ups and older boys like him better if he didn't take these clothes off? He wasn't sure, so, to play it safe, he took off the girl's clothes and put his own back on. He refolded the clothes as neatly as he could and went outside to find Skippy. They'd sit there together and wait for everyone to return. He would tell them that everything was the way they left it and that nothing strange had happened while they were gone.

Lost in the Woods

THE YOUNGEST BOY liked to read, but when he read, his mind jumped from the page and wandered off in new directions. When he read about a man who lost his way in the woods, he thought about a fish swimming from a creek into a river that went all the way into an ocean where there was so much water that the fish didn't know where it was. He felt sad for the fish who was lost in the ocean. What would that be like? He had seen pictures of the ocean and knew that it had so much water that it wouldn't make any difference which way the fish turned. Everything would look the same. When everything looks the same, what is a fish to do?

He went back to reading about the man who lost his way in the woods. The woods were different from the ocean. If the man was lost in the woods, he could tie a ribbon to a tree so he could remember it if he came that way again. That is exactly what the man did who was lost in the woods. The man in the woods also had a compass that the youngest boy was sure would help him as the story went along. Meanwhile, his fish didn't have a compass and wouldn't be able to tie a ribbon to a wave to remember where it had been. The fish was a lot worse off than the man who was lost in the woods.

"What are you reading?" asked a grown-up who saw the youngest boy reading.

"I'm reading about a fish lost in the woods," he said.

"Really?" said the grown-up. "How will the fish find its way out of the woods?"

"It's not going to be easy," said the youngest boy. "But I haven't read that far yet. I'll let you know."

WHAT THE YOUNGEST BOY LEARNED LISTENING TO MEN TALK

YOU COULD GET a dollar apiece for dead jackrabbits. It had to be one of those big jackrabbits, no measly cottontails. The dead jackrabbits had to be fresh. They went to a mink farm for mink food. No maggots or eyes already pecked out. Maybe the rabbit fur and hide were also used to make things. Nobody said anything about that.

You could get five dollars for a dead fox, but it couldn't have big bullet holes in it. The man who bought them sold them to some big outfit that made fox fur scarves and maybe even whole fox fur coats.

You could get twenty-five cents for a pair of pocket gopher front feet. You had to turn those in at the bank. The woman behind the bars at the bank liked it if the pocket gopher feet were dry or in a bag with some salt. Nobody said what the bank did with the pocket gopher feet. Nobody said where the money came from that paid for the pocket gopher feet.

And you could get fifty cents for a pigeon. The pigeon had to be alive and you had to have at least ten of them before the guy would buy any. He sold them to some place in Texas that used real pigeons instead of clay pigeons at a big country club shooting range.

On the farm, the youngest boy didn't see any chance of getting money for any of those dead animals, but there were hundreds of very alive pigeons. He knew he could catch pigeons at night in the barn, and he knew how to lock their wings. You just had to hook one wing behind the other. Without their wings flapping, it was easy to carry them to a cage without hurting them.

The youngest boy took a flashlight to the haymow and went to work on pigeon catching. He ended up with just one pigeon the first night and two more in the next three nights. He kept them in an old rabbit cage and fed them a handful of ground corn from the hog feeder every day. This made them very tame. They'd ruffle a little and walk over to his hand when he came to feed them. They got so tame that they'd sit on his hand and look up at him with eyes that were as kind looking as a pigeon's eyes could get. After a long time of catching and feeding pigeons he had ten of them and was ready to sell. The pigeon-buying man who came with the five dollars and a net didn't understand why the pigeons didn't try to get away when he reached for them.

"Are these pigeons sick?" he asked.

"No siree!" said the youngest boy. He ran his hand over the head and wings of the biggest one.

The youngest boy got his five dollars. He watched the man carry his ten pigeons away in a cage that he carried to his pickup.

The youngest boy liked to think about those men at the shooting range holding their guns and being ready to shoot. His pigeons would just sit there waiting for the men with guns to feed them. Maybe his tame live pigeons would make the men want to use clay pigeons instead.

FINDING YOUR OWN FAUCET

ONE BIG CHESTER White sow had fourteen little pigs. The babies were a mixed batch, most of them spotted and a few of them white like their big mama. The youngest boy watched that assortment of little pigs fighting for their turn to get some milk. The sow was really big so she must have had enough milk inside her to feed all of her babies. Having enough milk couldn't have been the problem: she just didn't have enough faucets for all of them to drink at the same time.

While all those little pigs were bumping snouts over the faucets, the youngest boy stood outside the pen and listened as much as he watched. The sweet little grunts the sow made while she was nursing sounded like what real happiness must feel like. Little grunts of sweet contentment.

What was going on inside the sow's head under those big ears while her babies were nursing her—or at least trying to? How did she make her grunts sound like music? The youngest boy tried to make the happy sounds the sow was making. He couldn't get close. Those sounds of nursing happiness were all hers.

But what about those fourteen little pigs, pushing and shoving and sometimes squealing and biting to get some milk from their happy, grunting mother? That must have been her secret: finding her own happiness and not worrying too much about how others found the happiness faucet they were looking for.

SKIPPY'S TAIL

THE JOKE the men liked to tell was that they chopped off Skippy's tail when he was a puppy so that he wouldn't be one of those silly dogs that was always chasing his tail.

The youngest boy didn't get the joke. That was supposed to be funny?

Skippy was silly in other ways that the youngest boy liked to see. He was a digger. He would dig in ditches, he would dig next to the barn, he would dig in hard dirt or in soft dirt. Sometimes Skippy would dig after something special, like an old bone, but most of the time Skippy didn't need anything to dig for. He just dug for digging's sake. His short little front legs would churn at the dirt, making clods spray out behind him. The mound of dirt that he made could get so high that it pushed up under Skippy's belly so far that he'd slide right into the hole he had just dug.

That was funny. But it wasn't funny in a way that the youngest boy could turn into a joke to tell the men.

What was even funnier is that Skippy liked to chase after his own shadow. One day Skippy chased his shadow in circles around the farmyard and all the way to the chicken coop. When his shadow got swallowed by the shadow of the chicken coop, Skippy looked at the youngest boy as if he had just won at some very big contest. He and his shadow sat down in the shadow of the chicken coop. Skippy looked at the youngest boy with a look that said, "I caught it!"

"Good boy," said the youngest boy and patted Skippy's head for being the first dog ever to catch his own shadow.

Now that was funny!

But how could he tell this joke to anybody in a way that would get them to see how much funnier this was than the fact that Skippy didn't have a tail to chase.

BETSY'S CALF

SOMETIMES IT WAS surprising what the men and older boys didn't notice. That day they didn't notice that old Betsy was acting like she was about to have her calf. Her middle looked as if it had a giant balloon inside, and she was looking back over her shoulder as if she was trying to figure out where some kind of ache was coming from. Most times when a cow looked like she was getting ready to have her calf, the men locked her up in a small pen in the cowbarn where they could watch her and maybe help her have her calf if things got tough. That's what happened last time Betsy had a calf. It took two older boys to pull that calf out.

This morning Betsy didn't walk with the other cows out to the pasture. She headed off on her own in the direction of the big dip in the middle of the pasture. It was a place the youngest boy knew well, because the grass was taller in the dip and if you sat down you'd be all by yourself with nothing but tall grass and butterflies around you. That's exactly where Betsy headed. When he started to follow her, Betsy looked back. She didn't like the youngest boy's attention, so he hid behind the fence until she got where she was going. He gave her some time and then walked over to the tall grass where Betsy was lying on her side and giving some big heaves to get the calf out of her. The youngest boy walked behind her to see how things were going. It would be fun if he would be the only person here when the calf was born, but he'd run to get the men and older boys if he saw that Betsy was having too much trouble.

Betsy wasn't having any trouble with this one. The little front hooves were already out, with the calf's nose between them. It looked as if the calf was diving into the world. And then, in one big slithery whoosh, there the calf was, slimy and beautiful in the tall grass.

The youngest boy felt like telling Betsy what a good job she had done, but Betsy was trying to stand up to see what had just happened. The calf's eyes were open, it was breathing, and it was trying to stand up too. Betsy and her calf stood up at the same time and looked at each other. Betsy walked over to what she had just done, sniffed her calf, and licked it behind the ears. The youngest boy saw that the legs of the calf and Betsy were shaking. He looked down. His legs were shaking too.

HIDE-AND-SEEK

THE OLDER BOYS taught the youngest boy how to play hide-and-seek. The rules were pretty easy. The seeker had to close his eyes and count to one hundred while the hiders ran away to hide. The first hider that the seeker found was the loser and would have to be the seeker next time. The last hider that the seeker found was the winner, but he didn't get much, except the fun of being able to say, "Ha ha, I won."

The boys drew straws to see who had to be the seeker. Somehow, the older boys made sure the youngest boy always got the shortest straw and had to be the seeker.

The older boys were mean, that was for sure, but the youngest boy thought that maybe they were also a little bit stupid. When they told the youngest boy to put his hands over his eyes while he counted because they thought he wouldn't really follow the rules and close his eyes when he counted, the youngest boy said, "All right" and put his hands over his eyes and started counting. Then he counted to one hundred so loud and so fast that the hiders took off running and didn't have time to notice that Skippy was watching where they were going. When the youngest boy finished counting, he looked at Skippy. With his nose, Skippy told him exactly where the older boys had run off to hide.

That's when the real fun started for the youngest boy. When he got to one hundred, he yelled, "Here I come, ready or not!" and walked in the opposite direction of where Skippy had already told him that the hiders were hiding.

He walked to the house and got a cookie from the cookie jar. When he came back out, between bites of his cookie, he yelled in a sad voice, "I can't find you! Give me a hint!"

When the hiders whistled and groaned, he yelled, "Louder! I still can't find you!"

The older-boy hiders lost their patience and yelled, "Over here, over here!" but the youngest boy pretended to hear voices from the opposite direction and walked away from the yelling. Skippy walked with the youngest boy and didn't give away the fact that they knew where the older boys were hiding. After about ten minutes of this game, the hiders came out of hiding and walked toward the youngest boy with mean looks on their faces.

"I see all of you at the same time!" yelled the youngest boy. "Now all of you have to be the seekers and I'll go off to hide. Count to one hundred, and no peeking."

The youngest boy looked down at Skippy. Skippy's stubby little tail wagged. That little dog knew they were in on this together and was enjoying it as much as the youngest boy was.

THE ARGUMENT

O N SOME SUNNY afternoons the youngest boy's daydreams seemed so real that he thought they really were real, like the time the pointed green leaves in the cornfield lifted a moon up above the corn tassels and held it there shining like an empty white saucer. That was real. And then there was the time when a small wispy cloud curled into a big grin against the blue sky at the same time that another cloud held out an arm and waved. That was real. But the daydream that wouldn't go away and got more and more real every second was of two boys about his age who stood in front of the red barn arguing and pointing their fingers at each other. Their words to each other were clear and real too. The one in the polka-dot shirt said, "I know how to count to a hundred million."

The other boy, the one in the blue shirt who had a flat-top butch haircut that stood up on his big head like oats stubble, said, "Why would you want to count to a hundred million, that's dumb."

"You can't count to a hundred million," said the polka-dot boy. "You're the dumb one."

The youngest boy wanted to put an end to their argument, so he pointed at the boys and said to Skippy, who was standing right there, "Sic 'em, Skippy."

Skippy looked at the spot where the youngest boy pointed and barked ten sharp barks in that direction.

That scared the two arguing daydream boys and they ran away. But these weren't the kind of boys who would be gone for long. Next time, the youngest boy would talk to them and ask them if maybe they'd like to go play in the haymow before they started one of their stupid arguments.

GARBAGE

ANYTHING THE PIGS wouldn't eat or that couldn't be burned in the trash barrel got thrown into the big ditch along the railroad track. The big ditch could flood in the spring but it still swallowed bottles and cans, old wood scraps and tarpaper, parts of worn-out tricycles and wagons, even a dead chicken now and then. All that garbage didn't slow the trains down, and it didn't spill over into the corn and oats fields, so nobody cared if someone added more garbage. When winter came, it all got covered with snow, and when summer came, weeds and cattails and tall grass shot up and hid the garbage again.

It was a warm summer day while the grown-ups were busy with whatever grown-ups do when the youngest boy decided to find out where all that garbage was hiding.

"Stay," the youngest boy said to Skippy. Skippy stayed.

And off the youngest boy went in his ankle-high shoes, the ones everybody called his work shoes, and made his way to the big ditch and then through the weeds and tall grass and cattails that were almost as tall as he was. In just three steps he could hear the garbage crunching. When he got to the middle of the ditch, he got down on his knees, pushed the weeds to the side, and started scratching. He didn't have to scratch very far before his fingers found a jelly jar and a ketchup bottle, then a tiny bottle that must have been for mercurochrome, and another tiny one that might have been for iodine. Those little bottles made him think of cuts and scratches. He slowed down

so that he wouldn't be the reason to open new bottles of mercurochrome or iodine. He broke off a cattail stalk to dig deeper. The garbage went in layers, maybe from different years of dumping. He got down to a layer of old tin cans that had turned into rust and then a little deeper where his fingers found a wooden box. He pulled it out of the gunk and tried to rub it clean with his hands that were muddy from digging. It was a pencil box that didn't look rotten at all. He shook it. What sounded like some pencils inside the box rattled around. He tried opening it, but the hinges were rusted and it wouldn't open.

He took his prize box of pencils to the tool shed. Skippy followed him and watched as the youngest boy put some oil on the rusty hinges. Then all it took was a screwdriver to open the pencil box. There they were, a handful of pencils, but they were mostly all used up and were nothing but little stubby things. They weren't pencils that had ever been his, but they still were pencils with some life left in them, even though not one of them had an eraser left on it.

He was ready to run to the house and show everyone the prize box of pencils he had found in the railroad ditch, but then he thought, Wait! The grown-ups had thrown this box of pencils away. They thought they were garbage, and they'd throw them away again if he showed this pencil box prize to them. He took out one of the pencils and wrote "Poison" on the lid of the box. Then he took it into the grove and buried it next to a tree where he knew he would always be able to find it. He put an old cream can lid over it before he buried it. This way it wouldn't get wet and all the pencils would stay just fine the way they were.

Skippy had followed him and stood by watching. The youngest boy looked at Skippy, wagged his finger, and said, "This is our secret."

When he got close to the house, one of the grown-ups demanded, "What have you been doing? You're covered with filth. Go wash up and don't come in for supper until you've got those dirty hands clean."

This was the easy part. He washed his hands twice. He walked back outside where Skippy was waiting. He wagged his finger again and said, "Don't go digging that up when I'm not there." Skippy looked at him, but the youngest boy could see that Skippy understood. He knew Skippy would help dig up those pencils when the right time came.

When the youngest boy sat down for supper that night, no one asked him any more questions about his day.

MATCHES

THE YOUNGEST BOY liked to play with matches. He didn't worry about starting a fire where nobody wanted a fire. He worried about being caught snitching the nice wooden matches that hung in a little metal box on the kitchen wall.

The boy figured the matches liked him more than they liked anyone else. He watched grown-ups strike the matches against walls and against tabletops and against stovetops, and lots of times the matches wouldn't light on the first try. Sometimes not even on the second try. When the youngest boy managed to snitch a little handful of these beautiful wooden matches with their smooth yellow and red heads, he'd find a long smooth surface like the bumper of a pickup truck or the side of a barn. Then he'd wind up slowly and give a long smooth swing, like a good batter who doesn't need a homerun, just a nice and easy single or double. The kitchen matches always lit for him on the first try. He'd wave the lit match gently in a circle to watch the flame and smoke do their little dance. Then he'd blow out the match in a long breath and stomp it into the dirt where no one would find it.

Knowing how to light a kitchen match on the first try became one of the youngest boy's many secrets. If he showed this secret to the grown-ups, they would know how to get a kitchen match to light on the first try. But they'd also hide the matches where he wouldn't be able to find them. This problem of not knowing what to do with his match-lighting secret made the youngest boy snitch more and more matches. If this had to be one of those secrets that he couldn't share, at least he'd be able to fill his pocket with them.

THE SAFETY PIN

THERE WAS AN OLD WOMAN down the road who had only one arm. This woman had a big apple orchard and would go out there carrying a little bucket in the hand she still had left. When she got to some ripe apples, she set the bucket down so she could use that same arm to pick apples. The youngest boy never heard anyone talk about what happened to the arm that wasn't there anymore. What he did hear is that the old woman was deaf on the same side that didn't have an arm.

The youngest boy made his way through the ditch so he could get to her place and watch her picking apples. At least he wouldn't have to worry that she'd hear him coming. And she didn't. Sitting in the ditch, peering at her through the tall grass, he thought he should go help her pick apples. And if he did that, should he use one of his good arms and hand to carry her bucket or should he use one of his good arms and hand to pick apples for her? Or should he use both of his good arms and hands, one to carry the bucket and one to pick her apples? He couldn't decide, so he just crawled out of the ditch, walked up to her close enough so that she could hear him, and asked, "Can I help you?"

That was a mistake. The old woman said, "Do I look like I need help? Let me alone. I'm doing just fine."

The youngest boy left, but that didn't mean he wouldn't return to watch her from the ditch. And he did. The next time he watched her, he noticed that she always wore a shirt that covered the bulge on her shoulder where an arm

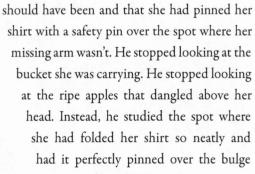

should have been and that she had pinned her shirt with a safety pin over the spot where her missing arm wasn't. He stopped looking at the bucket she was carrying. He stopped looking at the ripe apples that dangled above her head. Instead, he studied the spot where she had folded her shirt so neatly and had it perfectly pinned over the bulge where her missing arm must have started at one time. How on earth did she get that safety pin in her shirt like that? He remembered what she said to him the last time he asked her a question. He wasn't going to do that again. Carrying her bucket and putting it down so she could pick apples was one thing, but putting a safety pin in her shirt so perfectly was quite another thing. He needed both hands to put a safety pin in anything. He wanted to ask her how she did that with only one arm and one hand, but he didn't dare to go ask her another question. He certainly would not ask her if she needed any help with that safety pin.

THE LITTLE CHICKEN

THERE WAS ONE small chicken in the chicken coop that the other chickens picked on. They'd shove her away from the feeder with their big stiff-feather shoulders. If shoving didn't work they'd peck at her until she had too much of it and she'd run away. She'd go off by herself in a corner or hide under the roosts.

It didn't make sense to the youngest boy. He knew that the little chicken was what the grown-ups called a "laying hen." The youngest boy saw proof of that every day when he found a warm egg under her in the nest where she went to lay her egg. Her eggs were smaller than eggs from the big chickens, but he could count on getting a fresh egg every day from the little chicken.

A whole wall of square boxes made up the egg-laying nests for all the chickens. The youngest boy's job was to gather the eggs from all those egg-laying nests and to put a couple of handfuls of fresh straw in each nest. Some chickens made a mess of their nests, even when they didn't lay an egg that day. And many of them did not lay an egg every day. Some would lay an egg maybe every-other day, sometimes only once every three days. That wasn't the case with the little chicken. Every day without fail her nest would have a warm, fresh egg in it. And she always left her nest so neat and tidy that the youngest boy didn't even have to put fresh straw in. After the youngest boy gathered her egg for the day, she usually got out of the nest to get some food and a drink. That's when the shoving and pecking would start.

One day the youngest boy left the little chicken's egg in her nest. When he did that, she didn't get out of her nest. And while she stayed in her nest the big chickens didn't bother her. Maybe they thought she was brooding and getting ready to be a mother. At least those big chickens had enough respect to leave another chicken alone if she was getting ready to be a mother. The little chicken would still have to get out of her nest now and then to get some food and water and would probably be picked on when she went to the feeder, but the youngest boy figured he could keep her safe most of the time by leaving her eggs under her for a few days so those big cruel chickens would show her some respect for a while.

The Dream

THE YOUNGEST BOY had a dream that he could fly. He flew over the barn and had to swerve to miss the cupola. The pigeons that were sitting on the barn roof didn't scare when he flew over them. He flew over the barn twice, maybe trying to scare the pigeons the second time, though when he remembered the dream the next morning he wasn't sure if he was trying to scare the pigeons when he flew over them again or just trying to get a closer look. Or maybe just to show off to them that he could fly too. In the dream he almost landed on the lawn and was ready to start running when he hit the ground, but he didn't hit the ground. He lifted again and this time flew over to the one-room schoolhouse. The windows were dark but shiny. He thought he would land in front of the schoolhouse and go inside to see what was in the teacher's desk. Instead the dream took him to the roof of the schoolhouse.

He landed there. In the dream he felt very comfortable sitting on top of the schoolhouse and looking around at the whole world. He could see farm buildings and pastures and alfalfa fields and cornfields for miles and miles. Sitting on top of the schoolhouse, when he looked to the east the sun was rising and when he looked to the west the sun was setting. It never did get dark in the dream, but when he woke up the next morning he couldn't remember ever flying off the roof of the schoolhouse. He looked at the roof of the barn in broad daylight. The pigeons were there, just like they were in the dream, but they didn't look nearly as interesting now. In the dream they were many different colors, but now they were all the same dark blue. He walked over to the one-room schoolhouse. That was the same roof where he had landed in the dream, though he didn't remember seeing that missing shingle in his dream. Maybe I knocked off that shingle in my dream, he thought.

He sat down on the playground grass for a while and looked at the schoolhouse. There were a lot of books in that schoolhouse. He hadn't read very many of those books yet, but sitting there looking at the schoolhouse and remembering his dream, he felt as if he had read all of them.

BECOMING A BETTER BOY

O NE DAY THE YOUNGEST BOY woke up, looked at his reflection in his bedroom window, and thought, I am a very bad boy. I steal cookies from the cookie jar. I snitch matches from the matchbox. I lie about almost everything I do and don't do. He knew the older boys would agree with him. He knew all the grown-ups would agree with him. He knew it was time to change some things.

He started to make himself a better boy by pulling a cat's tail, then pulled his hand away quickly before the cat meowed or swiped its claws at him. The cat looked back at its tail as if it thought the tail might be the source of its pain. Then he went to the chicken coop, found an egg and threw it splattering against the wall of the chicken coop. The chickens saw the splattered egg and went pecking at it as if it were a special treat of their own making. He went to the hog house, picked up a newborn pig and held its little mouth close to one of its mother's dozen teats, then pulled it away just as the newborn pig was about to start nursing. He moved the newborn pig with its little clamp-clamp-clamping mouth from one teat to another, pulling it away over and over again until the little pig was about to give up, then put its little clamping mouth down on the biggest teat of all. The little pig looked really satisfied, looked as if it was taking credit for getting this big treat. He went out to the cowbarn just before milking time when all the cows were standing in a long row with their heads locked in stanchions. He walked behind them and grabbed the tail of a cow, gave it a good yank which made the cow kick, then went to the cow next to it and gave its tail a good yank which made that cow kick too. After he had yanked on the tails of a few more cows, they were kicking at each other instead of at him.

The youngest boy felt a lot better about everything after what he had done that day. He had taught himself that becoming a better boy meant learning how to mix up the good and the bad before anyone knew the difference.

BEING OLD ENOUGH

THEY TOLD THE YOUNGEST BOY that he was not old enough to drive the tractor by himself. They told him he was not old enough to swim in the creek by himself. He wasn't old enough to take a blanket and go by himself to sleep with the animals in the barn. Not even on a warm night. It sounded as if he wasn't old enough to do any of the things he wanted to do.

Then one of the grown-ups said, "Come over here, you're old enough to help butcher this rooster."

It was a young rooster, no bigger than a laying hen. He knew the neighbors butchered their roosters by putting the head and neck on a tree stump and chopping the head off with a hatchet. But there weren't any tree stumps on the farm where the youngest boy lived.

"Hold the rooster like this," said one of the men. He pressed the rooster's wings down hard and held the rooster like a big loaf of bread. The rooster's legs hung down scratching the air and its head bopped around as if it were looking for a place to run.

"Here," said the man. "Hold it really tight. I'll do the cutting." He didn't have a hatchet. He had a big butcher knife.

The youngest boy took the young rooster from the man's hands and held its wings tight against what would soon be the breast meat. The legs that would be drumsticks were busy running nowhere. This was worse than being at the dentist.

The man grabbed the rooster's head in one hand. When he raised the big butcher knife with his other hand, the youngest boy said "Whoops!" and let the rooster go fluttering wildly to the ground before the butcher knife could find its mark.

"Why did you do that!" demanded the man.

"I'm not old enough," said the youngest boy. He let out a false sob and watched the feathery streak make it to the chicken coop where it could hide among the laying hens. Maybe it could hide there for a long time, or at least until it was so old and big that it looked like the one that needed butchering.

COW PIES

THE OLD MEN TOLD of how once they would use dried-out cow pies to start a fire in the cookstove.

The next time the youngest boy went for a walk in the pasture he looked down at the splattered pies the cows had left on the ground. Most of these pies were still wet, and if you looked close you could see some of the kernels the cows had eaten the day before. What kind of person would pick something like that up and carry it to the house to put in a stove? He was glad he was not old. He was glad he was not one of those people who would bring a cow pie into the house. Into a place where people ate and told jokes and talked about what they had done that day.

The next time he was close to old people, he stared at them and listened carefully to every word they said. He didn't hear them talking about burning cow pies again, but he knew he had always better be ready to hear the worst. Who knows what other terrible things they might tell about how they used to do things?

Then he thought, No, those old people didn't get old by being stupid. A couple days later the temperature dropped so much that he had to wear a coat to go outside. He snuck a handful of matches in his pocket and walked out to the pasture. There were all those cow pies scattered here and there. He walked around the wet ones and found one that was all dried up. He touched it with the toe of his shoe. It moved and stayed in one piece. It looked like a thick crust of an apple pie with cinnamon sprinkled on top. He shoved it across the ground with his foot. It stayed in one piece. He struck a match and held it to that cow pie right there on the ground. It didn't light on the first try. He used a second match, and this time it started on fire, not a fast fire like the kind that happened when somebody poured kerosene on something they were trying to burn. More a steady, gentle fire. The flame crept slowly across the whole cow pie. He looked back toward the farmhouse to make sure no grown-ups were watching him play with matches. Then he bent down and warmed his hands on the cow pie fire. His hands got warm at the same time the cow pie burned itself out right there in the pasture. He put his hands to his nose. His fingers smelled good, like he had just washed them with a new bar of really good soap.

KNUCKLE CRACKING

THE GROWN-UPS TOLD the youngest boy to stop cracking his knuckles. Cracking his knuckles would make his knuckles get so big that he wouldn't be able to wear a ring when he got older. He noticed that people never wore a ring on their pointing finger, so he cracked the knuckle of his pointing finger on one hand every day for a week. Maybe five times a day for a week. The knuckle was still exactly the same size as the pointing-finger knuckle on his other hand.

So, why not? He went to work on his other knuckles. All of them. He became a master knuckle-cracker, cracking all of his knuckles three, four, or five times a day. His knuckles didn't get bigger, they just got louder. The only problem he could see is that the grown-ups might hear his knuckle cracking and punish him for it. Would he be the first person on earth to get a spanking for cracking his knuckles?

He wouldn't take the risk. He started making sure that he was somewhere where no one would hear his knuckle cracking. He had a knuckle-cracking good time for many weeks without anyone seeing or hearing his knuckle cracking. Then something happened that he wasn't expecting. Knuckle cracking got boring. The sound of his knuckles cracking got boring. Even that little popping feeling got boring.

So he stopped.

Sometimes he looked at his hands and imagined what they would look like with beautiful rings on them. Rings that he could slip on and off without having to force them over big knuckles. If he didn't like any of the rings that he could wear as a grown-up, he could always go back to cracking his knuckles.

WILD STEERS

WHEN THE STOCK truck unloaded the bunch of wild steers into the feedlot, the men and older boys did everything wrong. These steers had just come from some wide-open ranch in Montana and needed time to sniff the dirt where the old butchered steers had walked before they got here from Montana. These new ones needed time to get used to the grunting hog sounds from the hog house on the other side of the fence, time to get used to so many barns and sheds all around. What these new steers needed was some time to stand still and get their bearings. The last thing they needed was what the men and older boys were doing right then, shouting like crazy and waving their arms like it was the end of the world or something!

Waving their arms and shouting? What were those poor steers supposed to do? Nothing here looked like the wide-open spaces of Montana. The youngest boy had never seen Montana, but he knew it must look like a very long stretch of a whole lot of nothing, like a dead-grass lawn that went on forever and ever.

The youngest boy walked right past the men and older boys. Now they yelled at him, but he kept on walking toward those trembling steers. He stopped when he got close to them. He held out his hand and stood as still as they were standing. Only difference was that the youngest boy was not shaking the way all those steers were.

First one steered raised his nose at the youngest boy and sniffed. Then a couple more did.

The youngest boy aimed his nose at the steers and sniffed back at them. Then he held out his hand, not like he was trying to give them something, more like he was asking them for something.

One steer pawed the dirt with his front hoof. The youngest boy pawed his foot the way the steer did.

The rest of the steers looked on, but the youngest boy could see that the rest of the steers didn't trust him. That was all right. This would take a while, maybe a couple of days of coming out here holding out his hand and not shouting or waving his arms.

The men and older boys looked on. At least they had stopped yelling and waving their arms. They closed the gate and stood watching and waiting for the youngest boy to stop doing whatever he thought he was doing.

Fat Boy

ONE OF THE BOYS was fat. He was mostly bulges wherever you looked. When he walked, he waddled. The youngest boy liked the fat boy because he was easy to catch when they were playing tag on the playground. But then there was something else the youngest boy started to like about him. When another boy teased him, the fat boy never got mad. He aimed his calm eyes at the boy who did the teasing with a look of pity.

The youngest boy got that look once when he caught the fat boy at tag and said, "Gotcha."

The fat boy said, "Sure did," and then came that look of pity. The youngest boy couldn't hear or see a mean or sad twist in the way he said "Sure did" or in that look of pity.

When he wasn't being teased, the fat boy was usually alone. So was the youngest boy. The older boys liked to call the fat boy Fatso. They called the youngest boy a name too. They called him Measly Squirt.

It was time to talk to the fat boy about how mean the older boys were in calling both of them names.

When the older boys saw the youngest boy walking across the playground to talk to the fat boy, one of them yelled, "Hey, Measly Squirt, you better be careful. Fatso might sit on you!"

The fat boy listened when the youngest boy pointed out that both of them got teased a lot.

"They're just stupid," said the fat boy and gave his look of pity to nothing in particular.

"What should we do about it?" asked the youngest boy. "Should we tell on them?"

"Nah," said the fat boy. "Meanness finds itself."

The youngest boy didn't think he had the patience to let meanness find itself.

"The older boys always call me Measly Squirt."

"And they call me Fatso."

That's when they started calling each other Measly Squirt and Fatso in front of everyone. At first the older boys laughed and joined in on the fun. Then they got bored with it and started calling each other names. They called one boy "Moose Nose," another "Elephant Ears," and another "Bony Butt" and on and on like that. It looked as if the fat boy was right. Meanness really did find itself. The youngest boy started practicing the fat boy's look of pity.

VARIETY OF OPPORTUNITIES

A WHOLE BUNCH of town kids was going to visit the farm. This was their teachers' idea of a Field Trip! They chose the farm where the youngest boy lived because they heard it would provide "a variety of opportunities." Whatever that meant.

The town kids would be coming on a Saturday morning. The older boys didn't want to have anything to do with these town kids who thought they were so smart and liked to make fun of the way farm kids walked and talked. The older boys wanted to go to the roller rink in town while these town kids had their field trip on the farm. The older boys got their way.

This meant that the youngest boy would be the only boy left on the farm to show the town kids around. This sounded like fun. He'd show them what a variety of opportunities looked like. He dressed up for the occasion by wearing his Sunday suit and shirt and his black leather shoes. To top it off, he wore his wedding and funeral clip-on bowtie. Sure, this was a Saturday, but the occasion called for his Sunday best.

Four big cars driven by two teachers and two Moms unloaded the town kids that Saturday morning. Not one of them was dressed in their Sunday best.

They had on shaggy jeans with patches and holes in the knees. Grubby shirts with paint and dirt stains on them.

"We all got dressed for the farm," said one of the teachers. "We're ready."

The older boys had already left the farm for the roller rink, so one of the men pointed at the youngest boy and said, "He'll show you around," and then jumped in his pickup and drove away. Just like that, the youngest boy was left alone with these strangers who looked as if they'd been dragged through a garbage dump.

The whole bunch stood there staring at the youngest boy. They were like a congregation of lost souls who were looking at him as if he were a preacher who could deliver them from their scraggly misery. The youngest boy looked down at his Sunday suit and shoes. He touched his bowtie.

"This way!" he shouted. "And watch where you step!"

He had them. They were listening up.

"Over here we got the swine!" he said. He had just learned that word and liked how it sounded when he said it. "Don't get close to the swine." He waved his finger in a warning way. "They want to eat you!"

"Why are we here?" whimpered one of the town kids.

"Just listen!" scolded a teacher.

"See that there bull?" said the youngest boy and pointed at a moping old Hereford steer. "That critter, he's meaner than the swine. Not even gonna show you the chickens," he said. "They all got chicken pox."

Even the four grown-ups looked a little bit scared now.

"You gotta see the cows," said the youngest boy. "We call 'em the Kickers. And oh boy do they kick!"

The grown-ups were putting their hands on some of the town kids' shoulders. They probably would not be staying much longer. The youngest boy looked down at his Sunday shoes. He adjusted his bowtie. Everyone was looking at him, and they all looked afraid. So this is what it was like to be a preacher scaring a congregation with a variety of opportunities. He liked it.

PLOWED FIELD

THE YOUNGEST BOY was not big enough to drive a tractor, but he was big enough to stand at the edge of the oats stubble field to watch the tractor pulling the plow through the field. The oats stubble bristled like the head of a boy with a buzz cut, but the oats stubble was a dull color and definitely needed plowing over. The plow turned that dull oats stubble face-down and turned the black dirt face-up. Back and forth the tractor and plow went until the entire field was a lake of fresh black earth. So much change happening right there in front of his eyes!

But the youngest boy was not alone in seeing this big change. Seagulls swooped down out of nowhere, whole flocks of them, flapping and squawking and pecking at the upturned earth. They must have been finding earthworms and maybe leftover oats seeds. It was good to have the company of others who liked the plowed field, but where did the seagulls come from so far from the sea or from any lake? And how did the plowing news get to them?

PLAYGROUND TALK

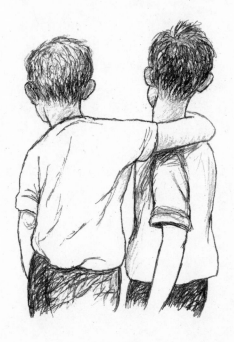

THE YOUNGEST BOY watched the older boys talking to girls on the playground. They were all smiling at each other. The youngest boy walked up to join them just so he could hear what made them smile so much. They weren't talking about anything funny. They were talking about what the other person was wearing. "You really look nice in that dress," or "That color really looks good on you."

What kind of stupid talk was that?

The youngest boy felt like getting into the talk and telling his newest why-did-the-chicken-cross-the-road joke that he heard someone tell in town Saturday night. But what if the older kids just laughed at him in a mean way? Maybe he should start telling some of the older kids how good they looked in their clothes. First he looked at the girls in their silly bright sweaters and skirts, then at the boys who seemed to think their T-shirts were really special.

He glanced down at his own jeans and plain blue shirt. Nobody's clothes seemed worth talking about to him. Not the boys' clothes, not the girls' clothes, not his own clothes.

He looked around and saw a squirrel sitting on a branch only ten feet away. Sitting on a branch and looking at them. It made little jerking moves, almost as if it were laughing at all of them. Yes, he could hear the short little chuckles coming out of the squirrel's throat. That squirrel was the only one around who was making any sense.

WHAT WAS GOING ON?

THE YOUNGEST BOY was in the shed with the baby chicks. The men had put up a heat bulb above a whole sea of little fluffy bundles of yellow fuzz. There had to be a hundred of them fluffing together and making the sweetest little peeping sounds the youngest boy had ever heard. They all were so much prettier now than they'd be after they grew feathers and started to look like chickens.

But something very wrong was going on. Some of the chicks were pecking at other chicks! Pecking them hard. The little heads and necks of three or four of them were covered with specks of blood where the pecking chicks had pecked at them.

What was going on? It was not as if they didn't have food. The men had a good-sized pan out for them with baby-chick food in it. There was a water pan too. The rims on the pan for food and the pan for water were low, even lower than a pie pan, so the baby chicks would have no trouble getting at the food and water with their short little necks. But some of them were still pecking each other!

The youngest boy got into the pen and flicked away the chicks that were pecking at other chicks. Why were they doing this? The feed the men had put out must taste a lot better than the blood of one of their brothers or sisters!

What they were doing to each other didn't make any sense, but the youngest boy figured that the ones who were doing the pecking just needed to be taught a lesson the way a puppy needed to be swatted if it chewed on boots that were left outside the front door. He flicked his finger at the head of a chick that was trying to peck another chick. This worked. The chick ran away and looked back, like maybe it knew it had done something bad and wouldn't do it again. That one didn't come back to do more pecking. But then there was another one doing the pecking. The youngest boy flicked that one too. And then another one that needed a good flicking. All the chicks were minding their own business and not pecking anybody when the youngest boy left the shed.

When he came back the next day to see how the chicks were doing, there were two dead ones, and their little heads had dried blood on them. He picked them up and put them in his coat pocket. He carried them out into the grove and scratched a grave for both of them. He didn't want the chicks that did the pecking to think that dead chicks were their reward, and he didn't want the men to see these dead ones either because he had told them about his finger-flicking remedy, and he didn't want the men to think that he didn't know what he was doing.

The youngest boy went back to the baby chicks. They were still pecking each other. He got in the pen with them and flicked the heads of the ones who were doing the pecking. He flicked a little harder. He would do whatever it took to stop this pecking, even if it meant ending up with a sore flicking finger.

Chicken-Salad Crunchies

WHEN HIS COUSINS from the city visited the farm, the first thing the youngest boy noticed was their teeth. They had nice teeth. Straight. White as the keys on the church organ. When these cousins smiled, all of those teeth were not just perfectly white, but the top and bottom teeth lined up with each other like two straight rows of corn with their leaves leaning over and fitting together beautifully. And their teeth had no gaps between them like the gaps between his own teeth. And none of his cousins had buckteeth like so many farm kids. The youngest boy didn't have buckteeth, but a couple of his teeth left gaps big enough to hold a kernel of corn where it would stay until he went after it with a fork or his fingernail.

All those nice teeth didn't bother the youngest boy nearly so much as the fact that his city cousins were so proud of them. Why couldn't they keep their mouths shut instead of smiling to advertise their teeth? Show-off teeth! Look-what-I've-got-that-you-don't-have teeth! Their teeth were so nice that they didn't even look real. Real things never looked this nice. His cousins' teeth were so nice that they were disgusting.

When sandwiches were being prepared for these city cousins, the youngest boy slipped away and got a handful of gravel from the driveway. He put a couple of tiny pebbles into all the sandwiches except the one he would be eating. His cousins would be getting the chicken-salad crunchies.

As his cousins chomped down on their sandwiches, there were some little snapping sounds. People with such nice teeth had to show good manners to measure up to the looks of their teeth. But nice teeth and good manners couldn't hide what was happening in their mouths as they politely chewed on their chicken-salad crunchies. The looks on their faces were somewhere between being scared and being ready to cry from the pain. Fair was fair. Those little bits of gravel were going a long way toward evening the score in the teeth department.

DAMAGED PEOPLE

THE GROWN-UPS DIDN'T say, "Don't do this" or "Don't do that." They just pointed at people who must have done something wrong. They pointed at the man with the missing hand who had tried to push a cornstalk into the whirring rollers of a corn picker. They pointed at the limping boy who had proven that he could jump from the fourteenth step of the ladder. They pointed at the man with a fingernail that was the color of the blood pushing up beneath it. That was the man who was always hammering something. He must have missed the nail. They even pointed at the boy with the glass eye who had leaned close to the sparkling welder without any goggles on.

It was a pity what had happened to all those people, and the youngest boy did look at them when the grown-ups pointed them out. What he needed to do was figure out how to do what those people had done without getting all that damage.

OATMEAL AND RASPBERRIES

THE YOUNGEST BOY looked at his plate. Mashed potatoes and carrots sat next to each other. The next night, red cabbage was on the same plate with very green peas. For breakfast the next morning, someone had sprinkled red raspberries on top of his oatmeal.

"I like this," said the youngest boy as he ate his oatmeal and raspberries. "It's really good."

"Glad you like," came a grown-up voice.

"And I really liked that red cabbage and peas we had for supper last night. That was really good too."

He knit his brow, remembering yet another meal. "And those mashed potatoes and carrots. I liked those."

"Everything is better when you have different colors on your plate. If everything is the same color, it's not as good."

"Oh," said the boy, and finished his oatmeal and raspberries.

When he finished eating, he went to his sock drawer. He put a red sock on one foot and a blue sock on the other. He folded the rest of the socks and made sure that they'd all be pairs of different colors. Then he ran out to the pasture with his different-colored socks on. The cows looked up as he came running toward them. One large Holstein raised her chin and aimed it at him as if she were about to moo her applause. The other cows turned their heads in his direction. It was clear they all could see that his different-colored socks had put a new bounce in his step.

SPARE CHANGE

THE GROWN-UPS TOLD the youngest boy that if he put away his small change instead of spending it, pretty soon he'd have a lot of money.

He practiced saving by dropping Cheerios in his cereal bowl one at a time. It took a lot of Cheerios to make a bowl worth pouring milk over. He did the same thing with kernels of corn. It took twenty kernels to make even a mouthful.

He decided he would go to work on the real thing. He had a nickel and two pennies left over from his week's allowance. The next week he held back on his spending and ended up with a spare dime. Every day for the next week he counted his spare change. It wasn't growing fast enough. He started looking down wherever he walked, just in case somebody had dropped some money as they walked. The farmyard was slim pickings. He found several shingle nails, but not one cent. Saturday nights in town seemed more promising. He was right. There was a nickel flashing on the street. Right in the middle of an intersection. He waved his cap in the air to let people know he was going out there. That worked. A big cattle truck stopped. The youngest boy ran out into the street and got the nickel. He waved the nickel in the air. The truck driver waved back and gave a couple of big-truck toots on his horn.

It had been a month now of finding and saving spare change. He had twenty-two cents. He started to think of what he would do with his money once he had a lot of it. A new bicycle came to mind, or at least a pocketknife with four blades. He started to carry his spare change with him in his pocket so he could feel the weight of it.

The next time he was in town, he checked out the prices of new bicycles and of pocket knives with four blades. He had all of his saved spare change in his pocket. He could hold all of it in one fist. This is stupid, he thought. He walked down the street to the drugstore and spent all of his saved spare change on candy. As he was enjoying the red licorice and candy corn, he thought, This is by far the smartest thing I've done in a long time. Smartest thing by far.

DEHORNING AND CASTRATING

MAYBE THINGS WOULD change someday, but what the youngest boy saw were steers with horns, some of them a foot long, being herded into a squeeze chute. The squeeze chute kept their whole bodies clamped tight and there was a stanchion on one end that would clamp their heads in place. This made it easy for one of the men with a saw to go to work on the horns. This was not like the dentist where you'd get a shot before the dentist went to work on your tooth. Nobody gave the steer anything for the pain. They just sawed away until the horn fell off. First one side, and then the other. The steer bellowed an awful sound and its eyes turned up as if it were looking for help from above.

Things weren't much better for the pigs, usually young boars no taller than the youngest boy's knees. One man would catch the young boar by a hind leg, sit down on a bucket or straw bale, put the boar's snout under one arm and pull the hind legs down on the squealing boar's belly so the man with that shiny castrating knife could make easy and quick work of it.

After all the blood and gore, after all the awful bellowing and squealing, what the youngest boy noticed the most was the look in the eyes of a steer that had just been dehorned or a little boar that had just been castrated. The eyes did not tell of the pain they must have been feeling. What the eyes said was "What just happened?" The eyes didn't even ask why. It was as if they thought knowing what happened would make whatever was going to come next in their lives a little bit easier.

When the youngest boy wandered around the farmyard, stopping to look at different animals that had not been dehorned or castrated, they recognized him and came oinking or mooing in his direction. Sure, they were just wondering if he had something to feed them, but he was pretty sure that they still liked him when he didn't have anything to feed them. They looked at him as if they thought he could make the rest of their lives a little bit better, whatever that might mean.

LEARNING A NEW WORD

THE YOUNGEST BOY learned a new word that summer. The meaning of the new word wrinkled across the grown-ups' faces when they said it. "Drought." They said it as if it were a bad word, like one of those words that would bring on the threat of having his mouth washed out with soap if he said it. When they pointed at what drought meant, he understood that some words were not bad to say but were bad because of what they meant.

The drought meant that all the corn on the hilltops was turning yellow and the leaves were curling like the fingers of the old man in the nursing home. The drought meant that on Saturday nights when everyone was in town people looked at each other as if the other person was to blame for nobody getting any rain. The drought meant that there would be only one crop of alfalfa because no fresh alfalfa grew back after the first cutting and that meant the steers would have less food and that meant they wouldn't grow very fast and that meant they wouldn't sell for as much money to buy things like new clothes and toys. It meant that wells were going dry and that everyone would have to use the same bath water so that there would be enough water left for the pigs and cows to drink, and if the pigs and cows couldn't drink then nobody would have any milk or meat.

"All the water has to go where it will do the most good," a grown-up explained.

There was still no sign of rain when the youngest boy went outside that day, and the burning sun was everywhere like a thirsty water thief. Just saying the word "drought" made his lips dry and made his tongue click off the top of his mouth. He wanted to do his part in dealing with this awful situation. He stood in the shade with his mouth closed. He rolled his tongue around, and soon new spit collected inside his mouth. He didn't know where it was coming from but he would save it until he had a whole mouthful and then swallow it all. Maybe if I always swallow my spit, there will be enough water left for the pigs and cows. He couldn't help the corn and alfalfa or the drying-up wells. They would have to wait for rain.

JUST PRACTICE

ONE DAY A FIRE TRUCK went by with its siren squealing through the air all around. Skippy heard it coming from a long ways away and stood stiff-legged with his ears up and his little nose pointing in the direction of the fire truck. Everyone joined Skippy in staring at the fire truck when it went by. Some of the men in the fire truck waved with big smiles on their faces. The youngest boy figured they liked fire as much as he did. Everyone followed the fire truck with their eyes and tried to see smoke in the direction the fire truck was heading. Nobody saw any smoke.

The youngest boy had to stay home while the older boys and the men jumped in the pickup to chase after the fire truck. The youngest boy and Skippy stood at the edge of the road watching the fire truck, and then more and more cars chasing after it. There was lots of dust coming up from the gravel road from the fire truck and all the cars and pickups that were chasing after it. This had to be something really big.

The siren stopped. As hard as he looked, the youngest boy couldn't see any smoke in the direction the fire truck and all those cars had gone. He walked down the gravel road kicking gravel. Skippy stopped and lifted a leg toward a milkweed in the ditch.

Pretty soon cars and pickups came driving slowly back. Then the fire truck came down the road too without its siren going.

"Did they put the fire out?" asked the youngest boy.

"There wasn't a fire," said one of the men.

"There wasn't a fire? But the fire truck. And the siren."

"Just practice."

Before going to the house for coffee, the men talked for a long time about the nothing that had not happened .

The youngest boy sat down with Skippy and tried to figure out what this all meant. Just practice? How do you practice with nothing? He should go snitch some matches and start something on fire. If he did, all those men could feel better about all this stupid practice stuff.

The Lilac Tree

THE FARMYARD WAS getting noisier every day. There was always the tractor that sounded off for almost any old reason, like a fence post needing to be pulled out or a cattle feeder needing to be moved. Tractors were doing what the old hired man used to do, and he didn't make much noise when he did his work. So the tractor was the worst, but then there were squeaking wagon wheels and the loose door on the old barn. Maybe all that noise was why the animals were getting noisier too. For starters, there were these two pigs who were always fighting to get at the same corn morsel in the same feeder. They could be a real squealing racket that went on all day. Didn't their mother teach them to share? The worst sound of all was the sound of the two Holstein calves that had just been weaned. It's not as if they weren't getting any milk now. They just had to drink it from a bucket instead of sucking it right out of their mother. So what was the problem?

"What's your problem?" the youngest boy shouted at the crying calves. "Get your milk from the bucket like all the big boys and girls! Grow up!"

All the youngest boy wanted on a warm summer day was to get away from all of this noise and find a little peace and quiet, someplace where his daydreams could float along without some noise spoiling it all. He walked into the grove to find a quiet place. He walked past the old cottonwood and past the box elder trees and planted himself under a big lilac bush. The lilacs were not in bloom any more, but the lilac bush's shade was a big promise of quiet. He didn't know a whole flock of sparrows would also like this big lilac bush. But they did. There must have been a hundred sparrows that had all decided on this lilac bush. Puffy little things, they all fussed around to find the exact place where they wanted to perch. It was nice and peaceful. Until one chirped. That one chirp spread like measles through the whole lilac bush, and in no time at all the lilac tree was full of chirping. The sparrows had turned the quiet lilac bush into a noisy tree. The youngest boy wanted to shout at them to stop all that chirping noise, but instead he put his fingers to his teeth and learned on the third try how to chirp back. His chirping surprised the sparrows. A few of them flew closer to him as if they couldn't believe where that chirping sound came from. And then they all chirped too. Not all at the same time, but there wasn't a second that went by without the sound of chirping, either his chirping or the chirping of the sparrows. This wasn't the peace and quiet he was hoping to find under the lilac tree, but being part of the chirping sparrow chorus was good enough.

Pigeons

THERE WAS SOMETHING strange about the way the pigeons flew over and around the house, over and around the chicken coop and over and around the hog house, but never landed on them. The only building where they landed was on the big red barn. The chicken coop and hog house were red too, so it must not have been the color.

The youngest boy studied the situation. Sometimes just a few pigeons, but lots of times whole flocks of pigeons settled down on the barn roof, and sat there for a long time as if sitting on the barn roof was like winning the jackpot of places to sit.

What did the pigeons have against the roofs of the house, the chicken coop and the hog house? The youngest boy already knew it wasn't the color because, except for the white house, they were all red. Then he figured it out: it had to be the size of the roofs. The roof of the big barn was like two great big tablets of shingles. Enormous tablets of shingles. Landing on smaller roofs for the pigeons must have meant more work. Of course. Pigeons liked the easy life, so they chose the biggest and easiest landing spots.

The youngest boy left the pigeons sitting on their big roof and went to check out which birds chose the hog house and chicken coop. No surprise: it was starlings and sparrows. It looked as if any place was good enough for sparrows and starlings. Starlings especially left a mess wherever they went, but at least the starlings and sparrows were busy birds who knew that life was not easy, whether it was in finding a place to nest or just a place to land and look around.

The youngest boy went back to the big barn. They were all still there, those pigeons, just taking it easy on their big shingle tablet. No wonder they made those *coo coo* sounds like happy little babies. The youngest boy sat down to look at the pigeons. They really were quite pretty, he could say that for them. But did they notice the chicken hawk that was circling up above? That chicken hawk was not looking for sparrows and starlings.

THE SALEBARN

ON SATURDAYS THE YOUNGEST BOY went along with the men and older boys to the salebarn. This meant a hamburger and malted milk from the salebarn restaurant for starters and then a ringside seat around the big sales rink where the cows and pigs and calves and sheep and sometimes kittens and puppies would be auctioned off to the highest bidder. The bidders sat in the big U-shaped bleachers around the sales rink that was big enough to hold about twenty five confused cattle or thirty five confused pigs or confused sheep at one time.

The youngest boy liked to get off the bleachers and away from the men and older boys to stand close to the sales rink for a good view of the animals that were being sold and to be close to the rattling voice of the auctioneer who stood with a microphone in a little booth above the sales rink.

"Bidda bidda bidda" he would start, and then that rattling voice that would say words so fast you could hardly tell what he was saying:

"Who'll give me five gimme five gimme five gimme five come on folks bidda bidda bidda, who'll gimme five gimme five gimme gimme gimme five five five hey! Who'll gimme ten gimme ten gimme ten gimme gimme gimme ten hey!"

Sometimes the youngest boy looked around at the bleachers full of bidders. He could tell that most of them weren't bidders at all. Many of them, especially the old men, must have come just to watch and listen the way he liked to do. They sat with their chins on their hands or were busy talking to other old men around them. The auctioneer's voice always sounded excited

even though his face looked bored with it all, and he didn't seem to care who was watching or listening, but he must have had a good eye because he could always catch the hand or nod of some bidder.

Then one time when the youngest boy was starting to get as bored as the auctioneer looked, into the ring came a very long-horned bull all by himself. He didn't look happy with anything. The way he stomped around the ring with his head down and those big horns swinging out like swords made the youngest boy feel great. Gave him the delicious shivers.

When the auctioneer said, "And here we have . . ." through the loudspeaker, the blasting words made that long-horned bull look up, aim his nose at the auctioneer and lunge up in one long-legged leap. The front hooves crashed against the plywood booth where the auctioneer stood. The booth must have been well built and didn't give way, but the auctioneer didn't start the bidding. He had two words: "No Sale."

It was the only time the youngest boy ever saw one of the animals come out as the winner in the sales rink. He wanted to clap for the bull as it left the sales rink in a proud hoof-stomping way, but decided not to. He hoped the bull would go off for a happy life, but he knew better.

Next into the sales rink came about ten of what the auctioneer called "feeder calves." The auctioneer's "gimme gimme gimme" voice was back at it. As the bidding started, the youngest boy kept thinking about that big bull. He figured that big winner of a bull would soon be somebody's stew meat.

STRAWSTACKS

BALERS MEANT THE END of strawstacks, those huge mounds of oats straw you'd see in feedlots or out in the middle of a field.

Cattle would rub against the bottom of one of these huge mounds and slowly carve little arched canopies where they could hide in a storm or go to scratch their backs. If cattle rubbed against a stack long enough, they made the stack look like a giant mushroom. Sparrows also burrowed into the stacks to make an easy nest that didn't require gathering sticks and hair and whatnot. All they had to do was peck and wriggle their way into a strawstack and they had themselves a nest.

The youngest boy remembered that when he was a really little boy he would stick his hand into one of those strawstack sparrow nests. The sparrow nests were deep as his elbow.

But balers baled away the strawstacks and made bales that were wrapped tight in baling wire. Most of the bales were kept in the haymows of barns. Huge rectangles of tightly bound bales that were too heavy for the youngest boy to lift. But the older boys helped him because they all agreed that the best thing to do with all these bales was to build tunnels. Which is what they did. Long, deep and winding tunnels. They stacked the bales so that there would be an opening big enough to crawl into. Maybe a tunnel would lead to a dead-end, maybe it would have some curves that led to light. With all the bales being the same rectangular size, it was easy to build all sorts of tunnels.

The youngest boy liked to crawl into the strawbale tunnel that led to a dead-end. He wriggled his way feet-first into a dead-end tunnel the way the sparrows must have done in the outside strawstacks. This tunnel was a lot deeper than the old outside strawstack tunnels, but it gave him the same warm darkness that the sparrows must have been looking for.

SIMONIZE

O N SUNDAY MORNINGS you could see these fat clouds of dust moving down the gravel roads as everybody headed for church after finishing their morning chores. That's where they were going too, and the youngest boy looked out the back window to watch the dust cloud fade into clear air the farther they got from it.

On the smooth paved road in town, he kept his eyes peeled for the man who was always standing on the driveway in front of his house and was not heading for any church. He was a gravel truck driver, and every Sunday morning he had his gravel truck and his two-tone red and white Buick parked in his driveway. He was busy washing them with that long black hose and a big white brush.

After church, when everyone was heading back home, the man was always still out there. He wouldn't have his hose and brush anymore, but he'd be holding a big rag and his arm would be swirling in circles as he polished his car and the cab of his truck. And did he ever know how to make that car and truck shine! The youngest boy stared at the glowing results of the man's work as they drove by.

"Simonize," one of the grown-ups said. "He should quit simonizing his truck and car and come to church to simonize his soul!"

The youngest boy wasn't sure what that meant, but when they got home he took a look at their car. It was covered with dust and some caked-on mud from last week's rain shower. Everything he looked at on the farm the rest of the day was dirty. The pigs' bellies had mud on them. Mud was stuck to the cows' flanks. Even little Skippy had gotten into something he shouldn't have gotten into. He not only was dirty, he stank.

"Come," he said to Skippy and took the little dog to the hydrant. The youngest boy ran just enough water into the bucket so that he'd still be able to carry it to the lawn. That's where Skippy's bath would happen. Skippy knew what was coming, but didn't run off. The little dog didn't like the scrubbing very much, but he liked being clean. The youngest boy washed Skippy and dried him off with a clean burlap sack. After that, Skippy was ready to play. Cleaning up Skippy made more sense than sitting in church for an hour trying to stay awake.

NO WAY!

NO WAY was he going to gather eggs by himself again. Not after what happened last time. Not after the older boys tied a piece of twine three inches off the ground right outside the door of the chicken coop and then hid behind the corn crib and laughed when he tripped on the twine and fell on his face with six eggs splattering on the ground and on his chin and neck.

Why hadn't he thought of this sooner? He'd fight back with what he wouldn't do!

The youngest boy had just thought of a way to fight back that no one had ever thought of before!

NOISY ROOM

A S SOON AS he walked into the room of noisy grown-ups, the youngest boy wished he had stayed outside with the older boys. Problem was the older boys didn't want him to be outside with them. They said he cheated at the games they were playing. Sure, he cheated. Who wouldn't with those stupid games? He was just trying to make them more interesting.

None of that mattered now because he was inside at some kind of party. An aunt's birthday party or something. All the youngest boy knew is that everyone was talking at the same time. A whole room full of sound. Some of the faces looked excited: those big open eyes and raised eyebrows. Other faces looked like they were trying to figure something out. They stood there with closed mouths. They were all ears to what the others were saying. Their ears were like big open mouths. The youngest boy liked the ones with closed mouths and open ears.

But the all-ears people didn't take all that noise out of the room. The noise was a big cloud, like a big storm of sound. Didn't anyone notice that the sun was going down and making shadows of everyone against the wall? There were even shadows of moving mouths? Why couldn't they all just stop for a couple minutes and look at their shadows on the wall instead of all this talk talk talk talk talk!

EYES

THERE WERE EYES everywhere! Those beady little flashes of black from the sparrow eyes in the trees—and then again in the middle of the farmyard where they were busy pecking at seeds or ruffling in the dust. At the hog feeders, the pigs lifted their snouts, and under their ears were those eyelashes that looked like the eyelashes of people. And then there were the pigeons. A dozen of them flew off the barn roof and found some crumbles of grain near the corncrib. Even though their eyes popped out on the sides of their heads, it was as if those eyes were in the backs of their heads. They turned their heads quickly—which meant that they had already seen the youngest boy. The barn swallows were another story. They proved how good their eyes were by swooping down within a foot of his head. They must have used their little eyes to guess how close they could come to his head in their swooping teasing way. He'd see their beautiful pointed wings but never their eyes. Maybe they just used those wings to hide their eyes.

When he walked into the cowbarn, Skippy and the cats were lounging around in the alleyway. All their eyes looked up at him, then looked down and closed as they went back to their naps in their soft beds of hay. But there were all the cows with their heads locked in their stanchions and facing the alleyway where he walked. Of all the eyes on the farm, he liked the cows' eyes the best. All those big peaceful cow eyes.

The youngest boy breathed with the cow, slow and steady, but this didn't change the eyes. The big dark eyes of the cow didn't look like they were trying to hide anything. They were like a blank tablet where he could scribble any-thing. They stayed steady, like a long question mark, but he could tell from the way they were mildly chewing their cuds in their easy chewing way that everything in their world was just fine with them. When he leaned close to look into one of those big eyes, the cow did not stutter or flinch. The big eye looked back at him like a mirror. Looking into that eye, he could see his own face. He leaned closer to get a bigger reflection of his own eye. When he did, his own jaw relaxed so much that it made him think that if he had a cud, he'd chew it too.

THINKING SKIPPY
TO DO THINGS

THE YOUNGEST BOY thought he could get Skippy to do anything just by looking at him and thinking of the thing he wanted Skippy to do. Skippy was sitting in the alleyway of the barn. The youngest boy looked at him and thought, "Lie down, Skippy."

It didn't work. Skippy noticed that he was being stared at and stared back.

The youngest boy scratched his ear, then thought, "Skippy, stand up." That didn't work either, but at least he had Skippy's attention. Skippy watched the youngest boy as he scratched his ear again, then stood up and walked toward the youngest boy as if he wanted something to eat. The youngest boy did have a dog treat in his pocket, a little dog biscuit he was saving for a time when he might want Skippy to come with him somewhere. He gave Skippy the dog biscuit.

Now Skippy walked away and stopped just when he got to the door of the barn. He looked back at the youngest boy, sat down and stared at the youngest boy. The youngest boy scratched his ear again, and then walked over to the door to let Skippy out. Together they walked out to the grove to Skippy's favorite spot to dig in the dirt for a while.

THE GRINNERS

WHY WERE THE OLDER BOYS always grinning when they looked at the youngest boy? If they saw him tying his shoes, they grinned. They grinned at him for the way he ate a piece of bread. If he climbed up on one of the low branches of a box elder tree, they grinned. Sometimes chuckles followed the grinning. The older boys acted as if he was their joke, no matter what he was doing.

In town on Saturday night, the youngest boy liked seeing so many faces of people who didn't grin when they looked at him. He tried to get these strangers' attention by walking a wobbly way when he crossed the street. A few people noticed him but none of them grinned. He turned around and walked backwards down the street and into a store. Some people stepped out of the way but nobody grinned. It was as if they didn't even see him. They looked right past him into a store window, or they looked at the person they were walking with. Mixing up with all these strange people was like not being anybody. It was like not even existing!

The next morning on the farm, the youngest boy made a point of tripping as he walked across the yard toward the barn. He spilled some of his oatmeal on the table at breakfast. The older boys all grinned at him. There were even a few chuckles. It was good to be home.

More Matches

THE YOUNGEST BOY took a handful of wooden matches and walked out to the barn. He held the little stack tight in his hand as he walked. He didn't want them rubbing together and setting themselves on fire before he got where he was going.

In the barn he found a little pile of straw close to the cement gutter that was a cow's length back from the stanchions where the cows stood when it was milking time. The cows weren't there right now so he didn't have to worry about some cow mooing his secret to the whole world. He lit the little mound of straw. It fluttered but wasn't eager to burn. He stamped out the fizzling little flame and kicked the ashes into the gutter where the cows did their business while their heads were locked in the stanchions.

There had to be a better place to use his matches. He climbed up the haymow and scratched together some dry alfalfa hay close to the haymow door. This would give the smoke someplace to go. When he lit a match and put it to the alfalfa, the flames jumped right up. He pushed more dry alfalfa close to the fire. The new hay caught fire right away. He held his hands over it and rubbed his fingers together. He was getting some real heat. Some curls of smoke drifted out the haymow door.

This might be a good time to go to the haymow door and yell, "Fire! Fire!" That would get the grown-ups' attention. They'd yell "Fire! Fire!" too and pretty soon the fire truck would come with its loud siren blaring through the whole neighborhood. Maybe two fire trucks, one from one town and one from another. He could make this a day people would talk about for a long time.

But then somebody would ask, "How did this fire start?"

The youngest boy had heard about spontaneous combustion in haymows. He could say, "It must have been that spontaneous combustion thing."

He looked back at his mound of burning alfalfa right there on the wooden haymow floor. It was getting smaller instead of bigger. He'd have to throw on more dry alfalfa to get this thing really going. He stamped on the outside edge of his little fire. This left nothing but ashes under his shoes. He kept stamping and his fire kept getting smaller. Pretty soon there was nothing but ashes under his feet and there wasn't any smoke going out the haymow door anymore.

It was time to call it a day. He put the rest of his matches back in the kitchen where he found them. Sometimes playing with the idea of doing something really big was better than doing it.

It's Coming!

EVERYONE WAS TALKING about it. A big storm was coming. Biggest storm of the season! Fifty-mile-an-hour winds and more than a foot of snow!

In town, there were big lines at the grocery store. Everybody was filling their cars and pickups with gas. At the hardware store, snow shovels were going faster than free gumdrops. People were buying new boots. The drug store sold out of cough medicine for the colds everybody would be getting. They sold out of bandages for the blisters people would get from shoveling all that snow. They even sold out of Vaseline for the chapped legs from being out there in the terrible storm. New mittens. New scarves. Warmer caps. New board games and 1000-piece jigsaw puzzles were sold. At least the people who owned those stores would have plenty of money when spring came.

People in town checked their storm windows and taped up any cracks around the window frames. On the farm, the men talked about turning the manure loaders on their tractors into snow scoops. No buckets or tools were left outside where they might disappear until a big thaw took off their blanket of snow so they could show themselves again.

Everybody was ready, but the big storm never got there. It petered out about two hundred miles to the west. People there were having awful problems, but not here where the sky looked gloomy but not mad at anybody below. So people sat around having coffee and talking about how terrible things might have been. The youngest boy stood at the kitchen window, looking out at the boring same old world where nothing had happened. It was like being at a birthday party without any presents.

Hooking Cars

In the winter when the side streets in town were packed with snow, the boys turned a Saturday night in town into a time for hooking cars. They'd stand at a stop sign and wait for drivers who looked as if they wouldn't care if boys ran behind their car, squatted and grabbed the bumper for a free ride down the snow-packed street. They had to plan ahead and find a street where the snow was packed hard for a long stretch so they'd get a good car-hooking ride. And they had to look out for bare spots on the road because hitting a bare spot in your rubber boots would mean your feet would stop right there and you could smash your face on the street.

One of the older boys said, "Better let go when you get to that green mailbox because there's a big bare spot right after that."

They all looked down the snow-packed street and saw where the big bare spot of pure pavement and no snow started.

A young man in a car pulled up to the stop sign. His big smile told the boys that he knew exactly what they were up to, maybe because he hooked cars before he was old enough to drive a car.

The youngest boy got a spot in the middle of the bumper with an older boy on either side of him. And off they went. The driver gunned his car and sent some snow and ice flying, but they were off at a good clip.

"Get ready to let go when we get to the big bare spot!" said one of the older boys as they went gliding along on the snow-packed street. It was like skiing without having to have snow skis!

Later, the youngest boy would not be able to remember the exact second when he decided that he would not let go when they got to the bare pavement. He'd just put his bottom close to the road and lift his toes so that he'd slide along on the heels of his boots on the bare pavement.

"Let go!" one of the older boys yelled just before they got to the bare pavement. The youngest boy hung on. He did not go splat on his face when they hit dry pavement. He skidded right along as if there was still snow under his feet. At the end of the block, the driver stopped and walked back to see the youngest boy still there, grinning.

"Holy cow!" said the young-man driver. "You crazy?"

"Nope, just wanted to lay some rubber."

The smell of burnt rubber hung in the air around them. To the youngest boy, it was the smell of victory. As he started his victory walk back to the older boys, the heat from his burnt boots warmed his feet. Nothing could have made this car-hooking adventure any better.

Statue of Liberty

THE IDEA WAS that no one would spend any money on Christmas presents. The idea was that everybody would make Christmas presents by hand for everyone else that year.

The older boys didn't like the idea because they thought any homemade present they got wouldn't be worth talking about. Maybe they were right because the youngest boy saw one of the older boys making a measly wagon with old Tinkertoys. Really old Tinkertoys. Whoever got that wagon as a Christmas present would have a Tinkertoy wagon with only three wheels. The grown-ups weren't doing any better. The flour and sugar on the kitchen counter told the youngest boy that Christmas presents from the grown-ups would be nothing more than cookies.

The youngest boy wanted to make a Christmas present that would be for everyone, a one-size-fits-all Christmas present, but it had to be something that would last a long time. Not like a cookie that is here one second and gone the next and not like a flimsy Tinkertoy wagon with three wheels. He wanted to make a present that people could enjoy for the rest of their lives, like the picture that hung on the living room wall of a girl bringing flowers to her grandmother. Or the picture that hung in the kitchen of the man with his hands folded over a loaf of bread. The grown-ups called those pictures works of art. That's the kind of Christmas present he wanted to make.

He looked in his coloring book and liked the uncolored picture of an octopus. He could color the octopus very carefully, staying inside the lines, even the lines of all those octopus legs. Wouldn't that be a work of art? But the grown-ups always threw old coloring book pictures away. He would have to make something that lasted longer than a page from a coloring book. He thought of the pictures he had seen of the Statue of Liberty. That was sculpture. Sculpture would last a lot longer than a colored page from the coloring book. Instead of coloring a picture of an octopus, he would make a sculpture of one.

The tool shed would be the best place to look for parts for his octopus sculpture. In the tool shed he found all kinds of screws and nuts, little strips of metal, and many cans that rattled when he shook them. His eyes landed on what once was a float for starting and stopping water for the cattle water tank. It was shaped like a big egg or a tiny football. Yes, this could be the body of his octopus sculpture, but he couldn't find anything that would work as legs. What he did find in almost every little jar and can in the tool shed was hundreds of washers of all sizes, like so many coins with a hole drilled in the middle, some as big as a half dollar and some smaller than a dime. He would have to make the octopus legs out of washers.

The grown-ups didn't let him use the soldering iron that used fire to melt the solder, but there were big tubes of some kind of paste that got hard as cement after you stuck it to something. He went to work cementing washers to his octopus float. He put the two biggest washers on top so everyone would know that they were the octopus's eyes. And then, instead of giving his octopus many long arms, he gave it forty metal washers all over its body. People could use their imagination. When he finished, he took a good look at what he had made. If anything could stand the test of time, his octopus sculpture could. He wrapped it carefully and taped a little note to the top of the washer octopus. The note said "Octopus."

At Christmas present opening time, he got the three-wheeled Tinkertoy wagon. He said he liked it. Everybody got a lot of cookies. When his octopus sculpture was opened, one of the grown-ups read his note: "Octopus." Everybody's eyes were wide open. He heard the words "Amazing" and "I've never seen anything like that" and "Now isn't that something!"

A week later the youngest boy's Christmas present was nowhere in sight. He went looking for it, and he did find it. Someone had put it in a clothes closet behind some clothes. He pushed the clothes back to see it better. Perfect. No one would hurt it back there. Like all those other works of art, it would last a very long time. Maybe forever.

THE DAY THAT SKIPPY DIED

IT WOULD HAVE been easier if Skippy had been sick for a long time. Skippy was never sick. He had his vaccinations. He never ate cooked chicken bones. He didn't chase cars that went by on the gravel road. Skippy wasn't one of those dogs that tried to bite the tire of a tractor as it drove across the yard. Lots of dogs died because they didn't have a lick of sense. The youngest boy knew that, but Skippy was different. Skippy was the most clever and cutest black and white rat terrier that anyone had ever seen.

"What a precious little thing that dog is!" people would say. Or, "My goodness, what a friendly one you've got there!"

There was nothing wrong with Skippy except for one missing toenail from a fight with a stray German shepherd two years ago. Skippy was only four years old and getting friendlier and friendlier with everyone, though the youngest boy was the only person Skippy could look straight in the eye without getting nervous. Skippy got along with pigs and cows. He had always slept in the barn with the cats, and they never fought.

Now Skippy was gone. Like the youngest boy's great uncles. Like the neighbor lady six miles away who got hit by a gravel truck when she walked out to the mailbox. It didn't make sense. The youngest boy sat alone in the barn talking to the cats, who were friendly enough and rubbed against his leg where he sat feeling sad.

Why couldn't the neighbor give Skippy one bad day? Skippy didn't hate chickens. Something strange must have been going on. Twenty dead chickens? That didn't sound like anything Skippy would do. But Skippy wasn't here to defend himself. What about me? the youngest boy wondered. If I had a bad day, would anybody give me a second chance?

AT THE FUNERAL FOR
THE MAN WHO KEPT CIGARS
IN HIS CAP

THE YOUNGEST BOY thought there should have been a lot more people there. Everyone for miles and miles around should have come to see him at what they called an "open-casket funeral." People were always telling the stories that the man who kept cigars in his cap told. Everybody knew his stories. Why weren't they here now?

The minister stood close to the casket in the front of the church. He looked down at the bristly and wrinkled face with a look on his own face that didn't say anything. The minister looked at the man who kept cigars in his cap as if he didn't even know him.

The youngest boy stood there remembering the stories he listened to in that little shed in the grove where the man who kept cigars in his cap would wash eggs with a kerosene lantern hanging in the middle of the shed. Wash eggs and wait for people to come and listen to him. The man who kept cigars in his cap had more stories under his cap than cigars.

So why weren't all those people here now? After all, this was his funeral. This was it.

The youngest boy didn't cry at the funeral of the man who kept cigars in his cap. He sat on the hard church pew puzzled. He didn't hear a word the minister said. He didn't close his eyes for the prayers.

He looked around and started to count the people who were at the funeral. He got up to twenty and then could tell that people were staring at him for staring at them. There weren't many more than the twenty he counted. There must have been hundreds of people who had heard the stories that the man who kept cigars in his cap told. Maybe they were all too busy working in the fields to come to this funeral. Would they all forget the man who kept cigars in his cap? Would they forget all his stories? The youngest boy tried to remember some of his stories. They were good stories, and he remembered laughing and sometimes almost crying at some of them, but now he was afraid he wasn't remembering them right.

After the funeral the lid to the coffin was closed and the pallbearers carried the coffin out to the hearse. Somebody had put that striped engineer's cap on the lid of the closed casket. That was the same cap where he kept his cigars. When the casket was set down behind the hearse, the youngest boy walked over to the casket. He leaned against it. He didn't care if anyone was watching. He reached for the cap and lifted it. No cigar fell out. Nothing fell out. The cap of the man who kept cigars in his cap was empty.

WHAT A BEAUTIFUL WORLD!

H E FINISHED HIS HOMEWORK last night and now, over an hour before he would be walking to the one-room schoolhouse, he had already gathered the eggs and put them in the egg crate. Nothing to do for a whole hour. What a beautiful world!

The morning sun lit up the rows of corn. The leaves danced in the crisp air—or were the leaves just growing? Either way, the corn would be much higher than knee-high by the Fourth of July. What a beautiful world!

He stood next to a box elder tree and whistled to the birds. His whistle didn't sound like any real bird's song, but his whistle made the birds wonder who he was. They came flapping and fluttering toward him from all directions. What a beautiful world!

A Hereford calf bounced across the cattle yard toward the electric fence, then stood frozen just a few feet from the fence, put its nose a few inches from the electrified wire and stopped before the awful shock. What a beautiful world!

But a little bunny must have tried to cross the road in front of a car or pickup that squashed it flat as a pancake. A crow sat over the squashed bunny, pecking away at the easy feast. Then the crow cawed for its friends to join in on the feast. What a beautiful world!

ABOUT THE AUTHOR

JIM HEYNEN GREW UP ON AN IOWA FARM in one of the last areas in the state to get electricity. He attended a one-room schoolhouse and graduated from eighth grade at age 12 before going on to high school, college, and then graduate school at the University of Iowa—and again at the University of Oregon. He is best known for his short-short stories *The Man Who Kept Cigars in His Cap*, Graywolf Press; *You Know What is Right*, North Point Press; *The One-Room Schoolhouse*, A. Knopf; *The Boys' House*, Minnesota Historical Society Press; and *Ordinary Sins*, Milkweed Editions). Minnesota astronaut George Pinky Nelson took a recording of Heynen's stories for bedtime listening on his last space mission. Heynen has also published three novels (*The Fall of Alice K.*, Milkweed Editions; *Cosmos Coyote and William the Nice*, YA, Henry Holt; *Being Youngest*, YA, Henry Holt), as well as several collections of poetry, including *A Suitable Church*, Copper Canyon Press, and *Standing Naked: New and Selected Poems*, Confluence Press. He wrote prose vignettes for two photography books published by The University of Iowa Press, *Harker's Barns* and *Sunday Afternoon on the Porch*. His one major nonfiction book, *One Hundred Over 100*, Fulcrum Publishers, featured 100 American centenarians. For many years he was writer in residence at St. Olaf College in Northfield, Minnesota. He has been awarded National Endowment for the Arts Fellowships in both poetry and fiction. He lives in Saint Paul, Minnesota.

ABOUT THE ARTIST

Tom Pohrt is a self taught artist who has illustrated more than twenty books, including *The Boy Who Ran to the Woods*, by Jim Harrison; *The Wishing Bone and Other Poems*, by Stephen Mitchell; *Careless Rambles*, poems of John Clare, selected by Tom Pohrt; and *Crow and Weasel*, the New York Times Best Seller by Barry Lopez. One of the first books Tom illustrated, in 1978, was *The Man Who Kept Cigars in His Cap*, by Jim Heynen.